ULTIMATE STICKER COLLECTION

HOW TO USE THIS BOOK

Read the captions, then find the sticker that best fits the space. (Hint: check the sticker labels for clues!)

•

Don't forget that your stickers can be stuck down and peeled off again.

•

There are lots of awesome extra stickers for creating your own NEXO KNIGHTS™ adventures throughout the book.

DK | Penguin Random House

Written and edited by Emma Grange and Rosie Peet
Designed by Jon Hall, Stefan Georgiou and Jade Wheaton
Jacket designed by Jon Hall

First published in Great Britain in 2016
by Dorling Kindersley Limited
80 Strand, London, WC2R 0RL

10 9 8 7 6 5 4 3 2
003–280401–March/2016

A CIP catalogue record for this book is available from the the British Library.

ISBN: 978-0-24123-223-1

Printed and bound in China

www.LEGO.com
www.dk.com

A WORLD OF IDEAS:
SEE ALL THERE IS TO KNOW

Each of the knights has a Shield Power that you can scan. Here is Macy's:

There are four other scannable shields within the pages of this book – can you find them?

THE LAND O KNIGHTON

Ruled by a king and a queen, and home to a group of brave knights and a wizard, Knighton is no ordinary land. Here, technology and magic exist side by side. Years ago, the realm of Knighton was nearly overrun by evil monsters, but King Halbert sought the help of the wizard Merlok to defeat them. And so Knighton is at peace – for now...

King Halbert
Gentle-hearted King Halbert is happiest when his kingdom is at peace. He likes attending balls more than fighting, but would do anything to protect his family.

Queen Halbert
Beneath the regal clothes, Queen Halbert is a fierce warrior. She knows how to wield a sword, and hopes her daughter will grow up to follow in her footsteps.

Princess Macy
Macy might not look much like a princess – because she prefers wearing armour to dresses. The king wants her to learn how to be a queen, but Macy wants to learn how to be a knight.

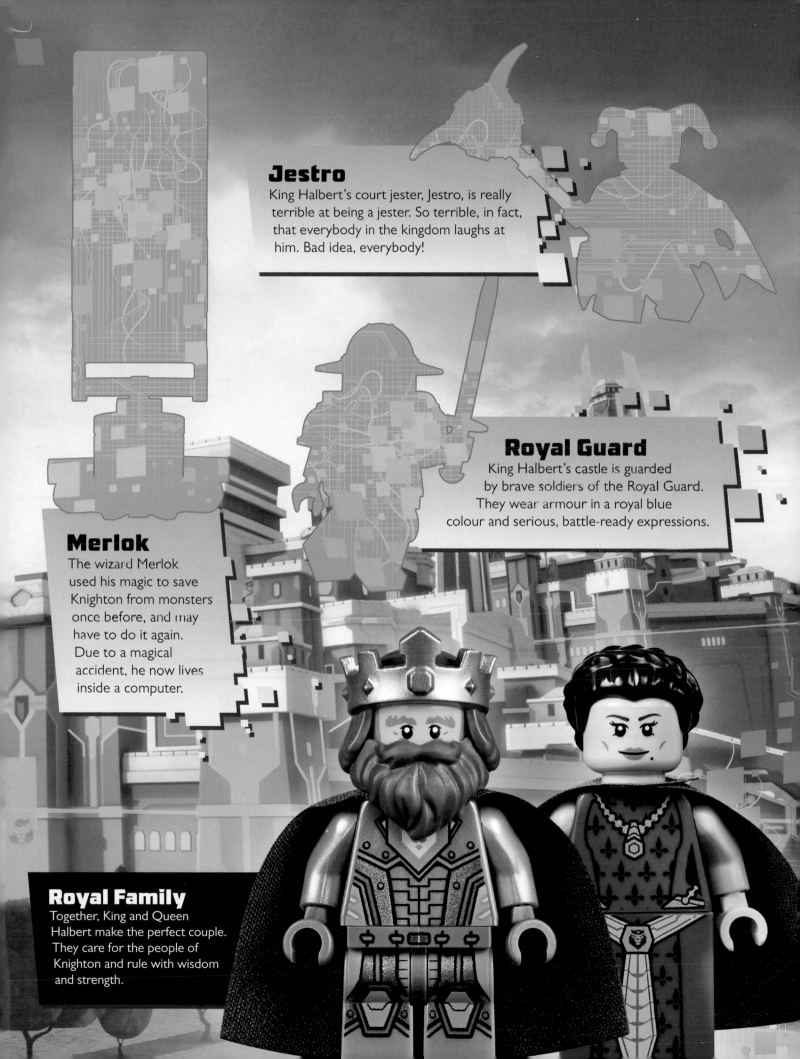

Jestro

King Halbert's court jester, Jestro, is really terrible at being a jester. So terrible, in fact, that everybody in the kingdom laughs at him. Bad idea, everybody!

Royal Guard

King Halbert's castle is guarded by brave soldiers of the Royal Guard. They wear armour in a royal blue colour and serious, battle-ready expressions.

Merlok

The wizard Merlok used his magic to save Knighton from monsters once before, and may have to do it again. Due to a magical accident, he now lives inside a computer.

Royal Family

Together, King and Queen Halbert make the perfect couple. They care for the people of Knighton and rule with wisdom and strength.

MEET THE KNIGHTS

This group of NEXO KNIGHTS™ friends have just graduated from Knighton's Knights' Academy. They are all different characters but they all share an eagerness to do battle with any beasts that might threaten Knighton. Here they are – bursting to go off on action-packed adventures!

Clay

Hard-working Clay takes being a knight very seriously. He studied hard to graduate top of his class. Now, he can't wait to prove himself in battle.

Mentor Merlok

The wizard Merlok teaches the knights about using their powers wisely. After being sucked into a computer, he now appears only as a digital hologram called "Merlok 2.0".

Ava

Young Ava has just started at the Knights' Academy. She is a computer whizz and an expert at technology. She works alongside Merlok as his apprentice.

Lance

Rich, famous Lance was the best jouster at the Knights' Academy. He enjoys being a celebrity and can be a little vain sometimes, but he is a loyal friend.

Aaron

Thrill-seeking Aaron loves taking risks. For him, danger is all part of the fun! He uses his NEXO Shield as a hoverboard to make battles even more exciting.

Macy

Princess Macy may be royal but she's just as tough as the other knights. She finds life in the castle boring and much prefers fighting monsters.

Axl

Axl may look fierce, but really he's a gentle giant. In his spare time he takes cooking lessons and plays the electric lute.

JESTRO'S LAIR

Peace in Knighton has come to an end. Jestro used to be King Halbert's court jester – but years of people laughing at him turned him bad. Now he hides out in his moving lair, called the Evil Mobile. This vile vehicle is equipped with everything Jestro needs to cause maximum chaos, and then make a speedy getaway.

Monster Minion

Jestro's hulking minion, Sparkks, has the job of pulling the Evil Mobile. He holds a frighteningly fiery blade in his clawed hand.

Evil Jester

His tattered jester's clothes, sinister skull pendant and twisted smile all give Jestro the strange look of a joke gone badly wrong.

Jestro's Plan

To conquer Knighton, Jestro plans to lead an army of monsters. He has found a magic book called the Book of Monsters, which has the power to release big, bad beasts into the land!

Driver's Seat

Jestro sits proudly on top of the Evil Mobile. He holds his magical staff, with which he can unleash all kinds of horrid beasts from the Book of Monsters.

Catapult

The Evil Mobile is a real mean machine – it is equipped with a huge catapult on either side, so Jestro can fire rocks and lava at his enemies.

A Lair for Loot

The Evil Mobile has a treasure chest secured at the centre, where Jestro can stash the loot he steals from Knighton.

Scary Face

The Evil Mobile has a terrifying face with glowing eyes and sharp teeth. It even looks like it's wearing a jester's hat.

Wheely Evil

Jestro's lair trundles along on two giant wheels. Their huge treads and perilous spikes stop anyone getting too close.

BATTLEFIELD

When monsters return to Knighton, the peaceful kingdom becomes a battlefield! Help the knights to save the day from angry Jestro.

Use the extra stickers to create your own scene.

MERLOK'S LIBRARY

Merlok thought that his library was the safest place to hide all sorts of magic books with dangerous powers. But Jestro found the Book of Monsters and Merlok's library was destroyed! Now the magic books are scattered all across Knighton. The race is on to find them and hide them in Merlok 2.0's new library before Jestro gets to them and releases their powers.

Flying Monster

Ash Attacker is one of the first monsters that Jestro releases into Knighton. With this flying machine he is on the hunt for magic books, too.

Computer Whizz

When Merlok's library was destroyed, Merlok disappeared. It was clever Ava who worked out that the wizard had become trapped in a digital world. From there he can send the knights special NEXO Powers to help them fight the monsters.

The Book of Revenge

If Jestro finds this book, he will be able to use it to create very vicious monsters. The Book of Revenge is coloured green for envy.

Window

Merlok 2.0's new library is kept secure by barred windows like this one. The magic books, such as the Book of Revenge, are safely stowed away behind it.

Leaping Lance

Lance wastes no time leaping into action to defend Merlok 2.0's new library, armed with his favourite weapon – which is a lance, of course.

Cannon

The library is equipped with two cannons that can shoot down pesky flying monsters in a single shot.

Fire Disc

A fiery spinning disc can be loaded into this slot in the library's wall. Ava uses her computer to fire this deadly missile at marauding monsters.

High-Tech Library

Ava's computer is fixed into the front wall of the library. From here, she can communicate with Merlok 2.0.

SQUIREBOTS

Squirebots are robots that perform all sorts of jobs in Knighton, from mechanics to chefs, and soldiers to butlers. Some live in the royal castle where they act as advisors to King Halbert, and some act as personal assistants to the knights. Wherever you are in Knighton, you're never far from one of these helpful robots.

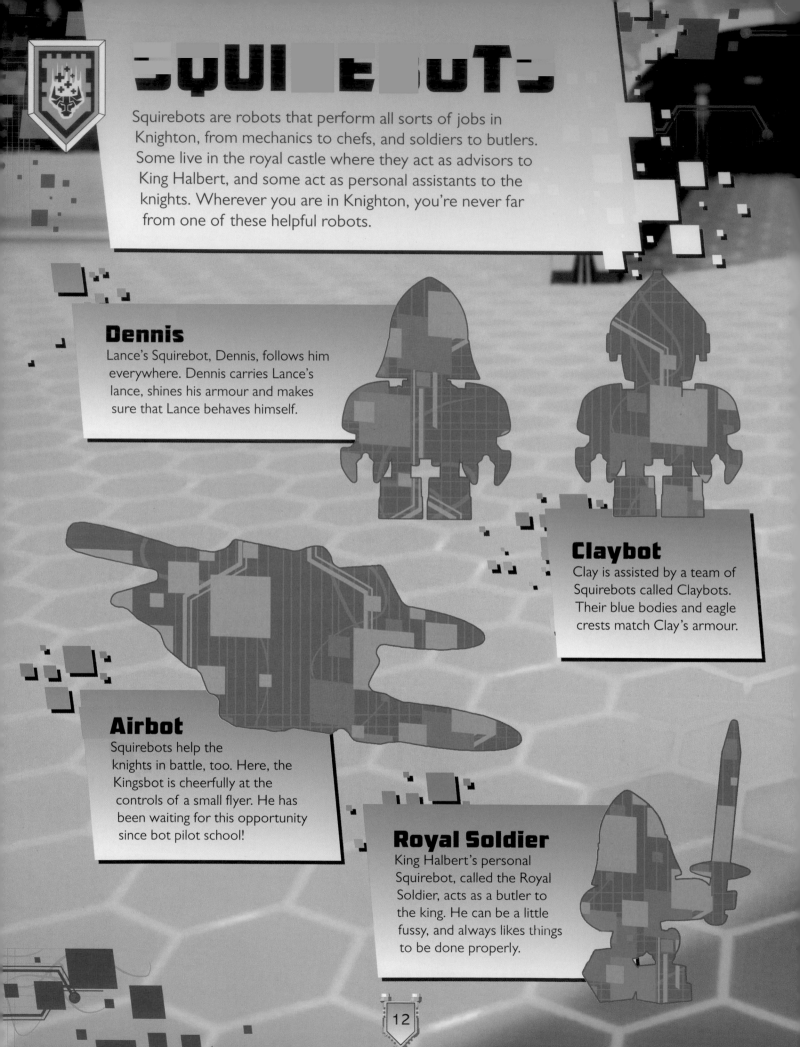

Dennis
Lance's Squirebot, Dennis, follows him everywhere. Dennis carries Lance's lance, shines his armour and makes sure that Lance behaves himself.

Claybot
Clay is assisted by a team of Squirebots called Claybots. Their blue bodies and eagle crests match Clay's armour.

Airbot
Squirebots help the knights in battle, too. Here, the Kingsbot is cheerfully at the controls of a small flyer. He has been waiting for this opportunity since bot pilot school!

Royal Soldier
King Halbert's personal Squirebot, called the Royal Soldier, acts as a butler to the king. He can be a little fussy, and always likes things to be done properly.

Motoring Ahead

This Claybot is feeling the need for speed and has commandeered this speeder. He holds a sword and wears a helmet with a face guard.

Chef Eclair

This gastronomically gifted bot used to work as the royal chef, but now Chef Eclair lives in The Fortrex with the knights, where he uses his talents to keep the hungry heroes well fed.

Snack Time

Axl thinks having a chef on board The Fortrex is the best thing ever, and always finds time to grab a bite to eat from him between quests. He is particularly fond of Chef Eclair's roast turkey.

ROYAL ARMOURY

The knights' mission to protect Knighton takes them into all sorts of dangerous situations. And no knight can embark on a quest without a strong suit of armour or a horse. In Knighton, vehicles, armour and even horses, called Hover Horses, are made from the latest technology. Now the knights and their king are ready to do battle with the fiercest of monsters!

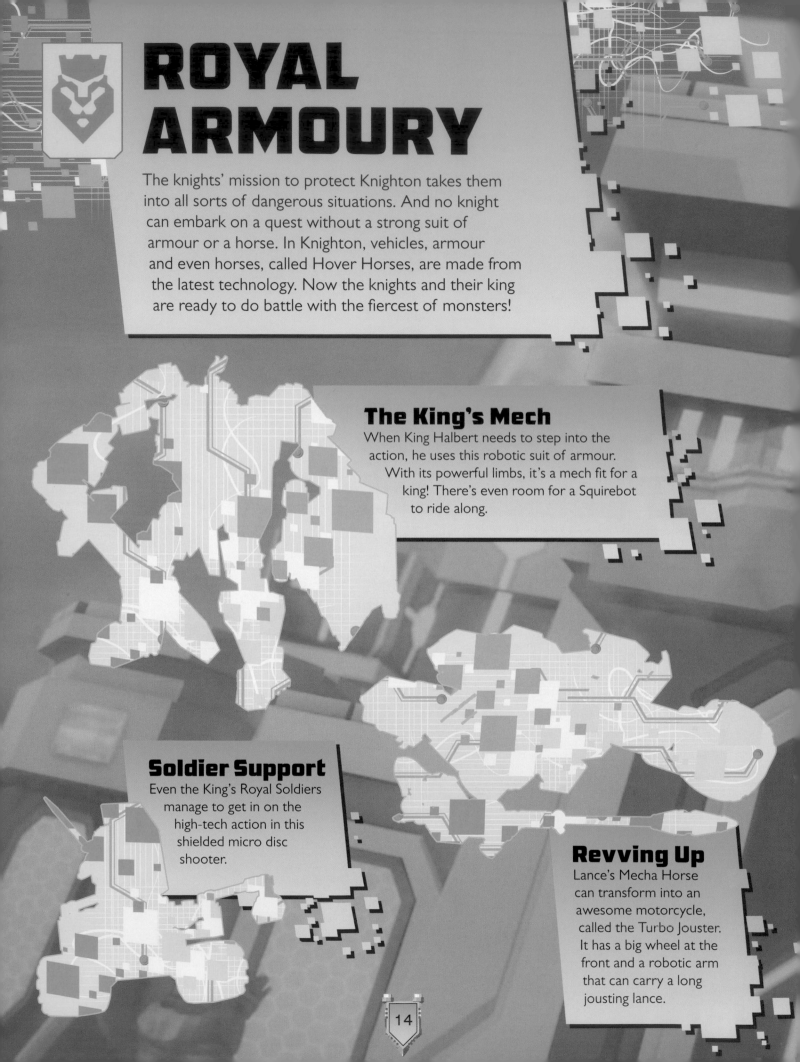

The King's Mech
When King Halbert needs to step into the action, he uses this robotic suit of armour. With its powerful limbs, it's a mech fit for a king! There's even room for a Squirebot to ride along.

Soldier Support
Even the King's Royal Soldiers manage to get in on the high-tech action in this shielded micro disc shooter.

Revving Up
Lance's Mecha Horse can transform into an awesome motorcycle, called the Turbo Jouster. It has a big wheel at the front and a robotic arm that can carry a long jousting lance.

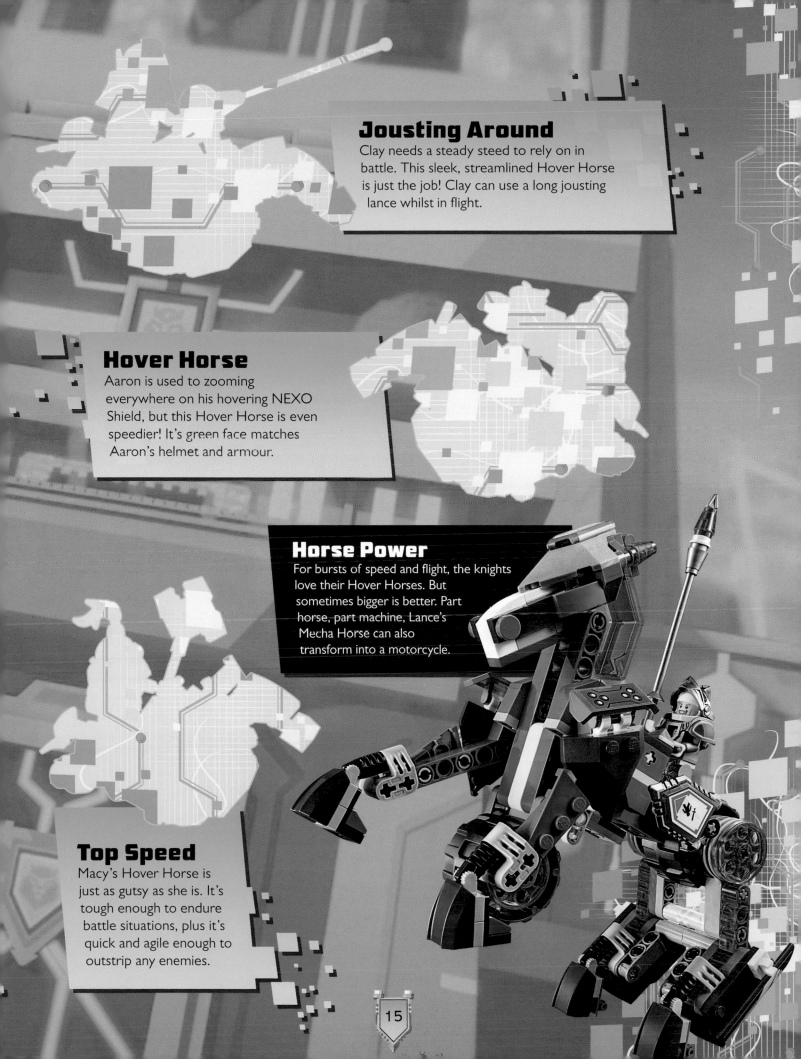

Jousting Around

Clay needs a steady steed to rely on in battle. This sleek, streamlined Hover Horse is just the job! Clay can use a long jousting lance whilst in flight.

Hover Horse

Aaron is used to zooming everywhere on his hovering NEXO Shield, but this Hover Horse is even speedier! It's green face matches Aaron's helmet and armour.

Horse Power

For bursts of speed and flight, the knights love their Hover Horses. But sometimes bigger is better. Part horse, part machine, Lance's Mecha Horse can also transform into a motorcycle.

Top Speed

Macy's Hover Horse is just as gutsy as she is. It's tough enough to endure battle situations, plus it's quick and agile enough to outstrip any enemies.

MAGMA MONSTERS

With a stolen book, a little bit of magic and a big, bad desire to cause chaos and get revenge, Jestro has managed to summon a whole army of evil monsters into Knighton! These creatures have a love of lava, fire and all things hot, and so are known as Magma Monsters. Jestro hopes they will help him to conquer Knighton.

Crust Smasher

Armed in spiked protective armour, the Crust Smasher is ready to run through fire and flames to launch a fiery attack on Knighton.

Ash Attacker

The catapult-wielding Ash Attacker loves to lead an attack. Like his fellow Magma Monsters, he is flame-coloured red all over, with blazing yellow eyes.

Infernox

Bumbling Infernox has big, crushing feet, but no sense of co-ordination, so is as likely to step on a fellow monster as an enemy knight. He is repeatedly defeated by Clay and his friends.

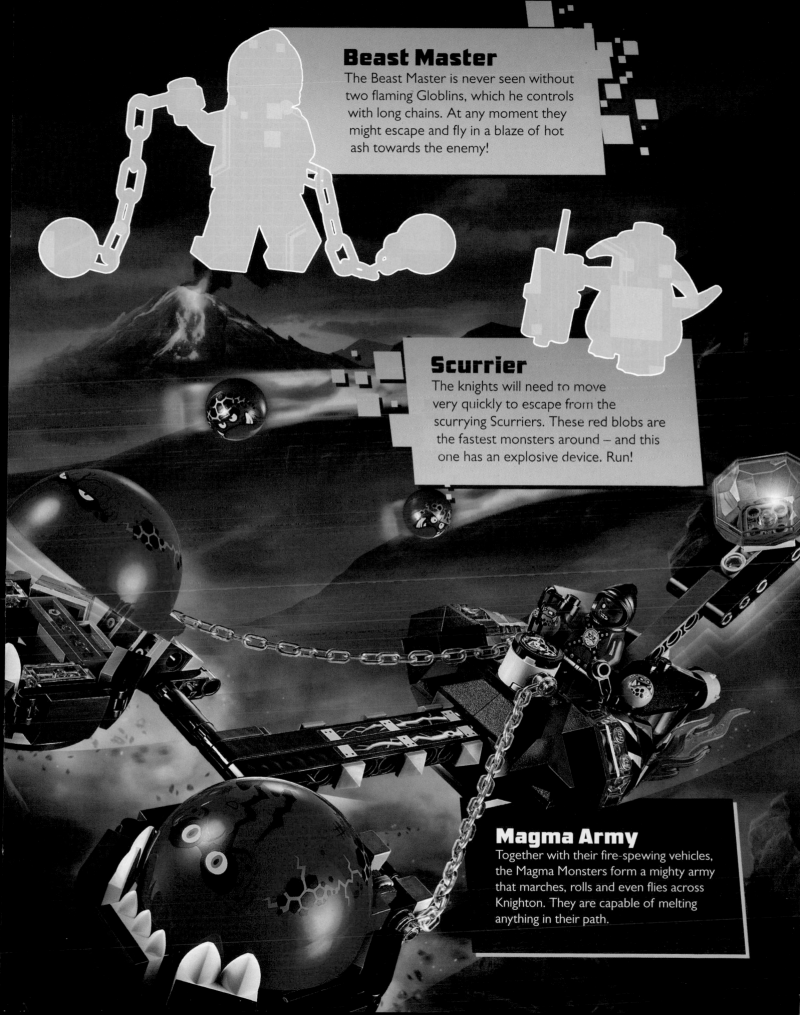

Beast Master

The Beast Master is never seen without two flaming Globlins, which he controls with long chains. At any moment they might escape and fly in a blaze of hot ash towards the enemy!

Scurrier

The knights will need to move very quickly to escape from the scurrying Scurriers. These red blobs are the fastest monsters around – and this one has an explosive device. Run!

Magma Army

Together with their fire-spewing vehicles, the Magma Monsters form a mighty army that marches, rolls and even flies across Knighton. They are capable of melting anything in their path.

MORE MAGMA MONSTERS!

Just when the knights think it can't get any worse, Jestro summons even more Magma Monsters out of the Book of Monsters! With these foes hotter than ever before, living in Knighton is looking increasingly perilous.

Moltor

Boulder-bashing Moltor has giant, crushing fists for hands, and rarely says a word. He could do some damage to the knights if he got his huge hands on them.

Mean and Keen

The wide toothy grin on this Scurrier's face shows just how much he enjoys a fight. Armed with a short sword, he's ready to take out the legs of any unsuspecting passing knight.

Flame Thrower

His spiky hairdo looks like it ought to be a fire hazard, but the Flame Thrower charges on into battle regardless. He loves the heat of a fight more than anything else.

Globlins

The Scurriers are small, but the Globlins are even smaller. Entirely unpredictable, due to their ability to bounce anywhere they choose, the Globlins like to arrive in fireball-breathing packs!

Ready for Battle

The Scurriers are rarely spotted without weapons clutched in their fiery hands. This spear will be useful for jabbing knights from behind.

Sparkks

Bigger than the other monsters, Sparkks is always apologising for getting in the way and not being monstrous enough. To Jestro's disgust, Sparkks just can't be as bad as he is huge!

Turn up the Heat

The magical Magma Monsters love scorching hot temperatures the most. They come swarming out of the Book of Monsters with lava weapons and dangerous, fiery tempers.

THE LAVA LANDS

Not much is known about the volcanic Lava Lands, apart from the fact that they're very dark and very hot! The Magma Monsters would probably like it here...

Use the extra stickers to create your own scene.

THE FORTREX

This rolling castle is the perfect base for the knights. Its towers are armed with revolving missile launchers – ready to take out multiple Magma Monsters at once. Inside, it's a place for the knights to rest in between battles. Coolest of all, the castle is full of high-tech vehicles and equipment, and is the home of Merlok 2.0.

Airborne Aaron

When monsters attack, Aaron defends The Fortrex on his Aero-Striker. It has a red lance on either side, and can shoot a missile that really packs a punch!

Knight Cycle

Clay takes to his Knight Cycle to defend The Fortrex. This speedy vehicle has two wheels like a motorcycle.

Onboard Chef

Inside The Fortrex, the Chefbot uses his saucepan to cook up tasty, nutritious meals to keep the knights' strength up.

Towering Ahead

The Fortrex has four towers where the knights can watch for enemies. On the front of each tower is a shield bearing King Halbert's coat of arms.

Plugged In

Merlok 2.0 lives within the walls of The Fortrex. He has complete control over the castle – he can even lock the knights out if he feels like it!

Rolling Around

The Fortrex has caterpillar treads like a tank, so it can roll across even the rockiest of terrain in pursuit of Magma Monsters.

NEXO POWERS

Merlok 2.0 uses super-cool digital technology and the knights' shields to send them awesome new powers – called NEXO Powers – that help the knights in battle. Some take the form of cool weapons, and others give the knights amazing new abilities.

Toxic Sting

Lance can use the Toxic Sting power to surround himself in a cloud of poisonous gas. No enemies can approach without getting a lungful of ghastly gas.

NEXO Glow

When the knights receive a NEXO Power, their weapons and armour are filled with a powerful magic energy, making them glow.

Backlash Lightning

With the Backlash Lightning power, Clay can fire a powerful bolt of lightning, which causes havoc as it bounces around the battlefield.

Rolling Fire Ball

Aaron has the Rolling Fire Ball power, which surrounds him in a sphere of flames. It leaves Aaron unharmed, but any enemies that come close get singed!

Clapper Claw

The Clapper Claw power gives Macy the strength of a fiery red dragon. The Magma Monsters had better watch out, or they'll be toast.

Ground Power

Now Axl can really shake things up! With Ground Power, a knight can smash their weapon into the ground to create shockwaves that stun enemies.

MONSTER MACHINES

The Magma Monsters have some lean, mean fighting machines that they use to unleash terror on Knighton. With their colossal catapults, weird wings and terrifying teeth, these ferocious weapons really help the Magma Monsters turn up the heat against the knights.

Lava Shooter

This Lava Shooter swivels on an axis, allowing the Magma Monster at the controls to take aim before firing. Two monstrous horns flank the controls.

Winged Flyer

This small flying vehicle has scary bat-like wings. The claw at the front holds a molten missile to be fired at enemies.

Lava Smasher

Moltor's Lava Smasher has two smouldering rocks that act as huge smashing fists – much like his own! The vehicle rolls along like a steamroller, flattening everything in its path.

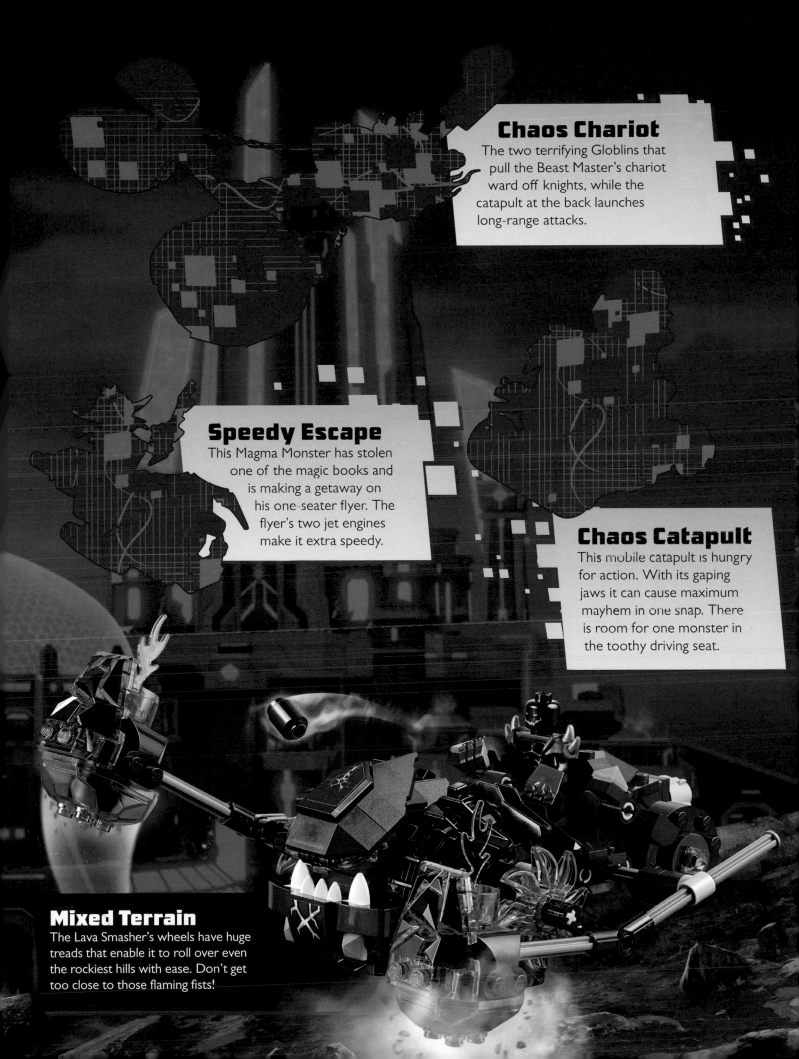

Chaos Chariot

The two terrifying Globlins that pull the Beast Master's chariot ward off knights, while the catapult at the back launches long-range attacks.

Speedy Escape

This Magma Monster has stolen one of the magic books and is making a getaway on his one-seater flyer. The flyer's two jet engines make it extra speedy.

Chaos Catapult

This mobile catapult is hungry for action. With its gaping jaws it can cause maximum mayhem in one snap. There is room for one monster in the toothy driving seat.

Mixed Terrain

The Lava Smasher's wheels have huge treads that enable it to roll over even the rockiest hills with ease. Don't get too close to those flaming fists!

INTO BATTLE

The knights and the monsters go head-to-head on the battlefield. The result is a mighty clash of NEXO technology and fiery monster weaponry. The knights must give it everything they've got! And luckily they've got a lot – an armoury of awesome weapons, and Merlok 2.0.

Rumble Blade

Clay's Rumble Blade is shaped like a giant sword. The distinctive shape makes it very aerodynamic. Clay thinks it looks pretty sharp, too.

On the March

The knights bring all of their best vehicles to the battlefield. Clay's machine can split into several parts, driven by his eager Squirebots.

Catapult Attack

Crust Smasher loads smouldering rocks into the fearsome, fanged Chaos Catapult and fires them into the fray.

Bot vs Scurrier

On the ground, a soldier bot battles a small Scurrier monster. The monsters are stronger than the bots and the Scurrier's sword is fierce and jagged. Who will win this fight?

Blade to Blade

This Royal Guard, in his blue armour, clashes swords with Crust Smasher. The guard, with his simple sword skills, seems to stand no chance. Will the knights come to his rescue?

KNIGHTON INVASION!

Knighton is a peaceful city, until Jestro and his Magma Monsters invade! The people of Knighton are depending on the knights to defend their city from the attackers.

Use the
extra
stickers to
create your
own scene.

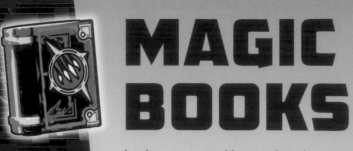

MAGIC BOOKS

In the average library, books are quiet and well-behaved. But not in Knighton! Released from where they were locked up under Merlok's control, this boisterous bunch of books runs riot – walking and talking and unleashing evil powers for Jestro. Their ringleader is the truly monstrous Book of Monsters.

Book of Monsters

This book could be accused of getting too big for its boots. The Book of Monsters has the power to release monsters and gains more powers by eating other books.

Book of Chaos

This little book can cause a lot of mayhem! Because of this, the Book of Chaos is the only book that the Book of Monsters does not want to eat.

Book of Evil

The first book to be found by Jestro, the Book of Evil is really, really evil! It helps the Book of Monsters to make very nasty monsters.

Book of Deception

When Jestro wants sneaky monsters that are good at disguising themselves, he turns to the Book of Deception. Look out behind you, brave knights!

Merlok

Toxic Sting

Ready, Aim, Fire!

Kingsbot at the Ready

Bot vs Scurrier

Smart Ava

Massive Monster

Monster Minion

Jestro's Plan

Royal Guard

Bot vs Scurrier

Royal
Friends

Driver's Seat

Dishonest Book

Plugged In

Book Thief

Four-wheeled
Drive

Prowling Monster

Princess Macy

Window

Armed with
Ground Power

Scary Face

Mecha Horse

Macy's Hover Horse

Red-hot Foe

Monster Mayhem

©2016 LEGO

©2016 LEGO

©2016 LEGO

©2016 LEGO

©2016 LEGO

Clay

Lance's Squirebot

©2016 LEGO

Queen Halbert

©2016 LEGO

©2016 LEGO

©2016 LEGO

Battle Macy

Armed Claybot

©2016 LEGO

On a Roll

©2016 LEGO

©2016 LEGO

Moltor

Marching Monster

Book of Deception

Lance

Missiles

Scurrier

Battle King

Armoured Aaron

Royal Racer

Chaos Chariot

Standing Guard

Wizard's Apprentice

Thrill Seeker

Hidden Treasure

Computer Whizz

Flying Monster

Guard in
Charge

Book of Evil

Wise
Queen

Kingsbot

Into Battle!

Armed and
Ready

Flamethrower

Cannon

Robotic Helper

Wheely Evil

The Book of Revenge

Airbot

Powered-up Clay

Flying Magma Monster

Aaron

Dinner Time

Evil Jester

Beastly Brute

King of Knighton

Claybot

Leaping Lance

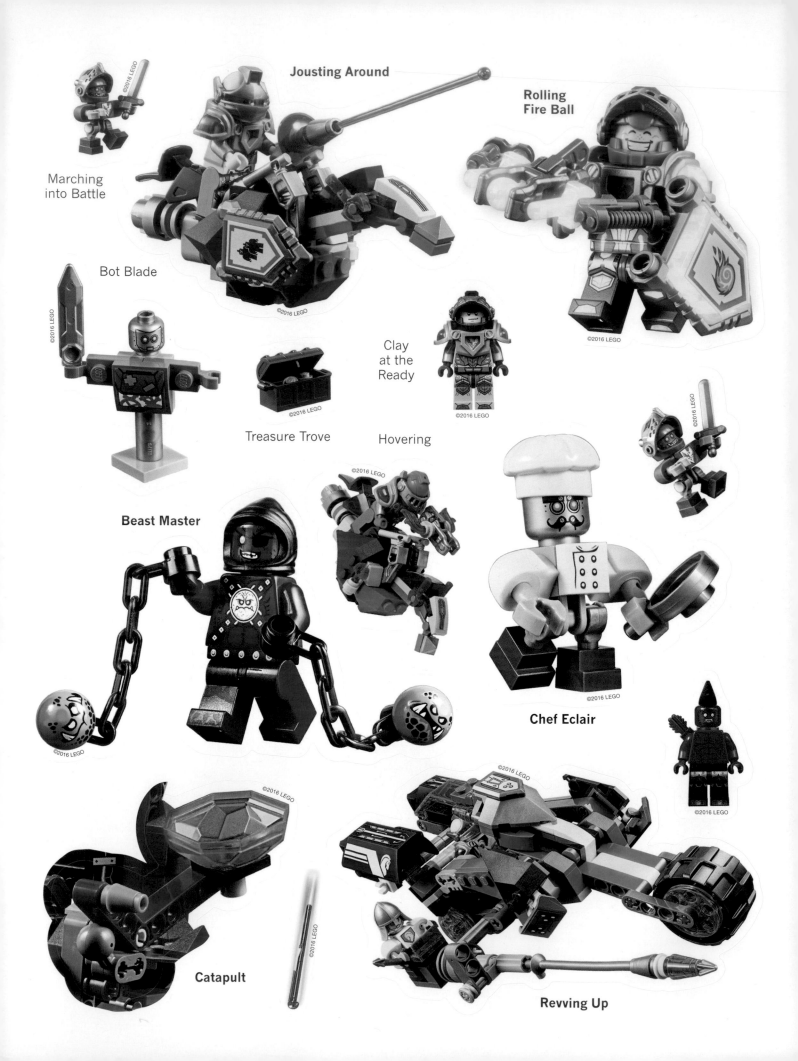

Jousting Around

Rolling
Fire Ball

Marching
into Battle

Bot Blade

Clay
at the
Ready

Treasure Trove

Hovering

Beast Master

Chef Eclair

Catapult

Revving Up

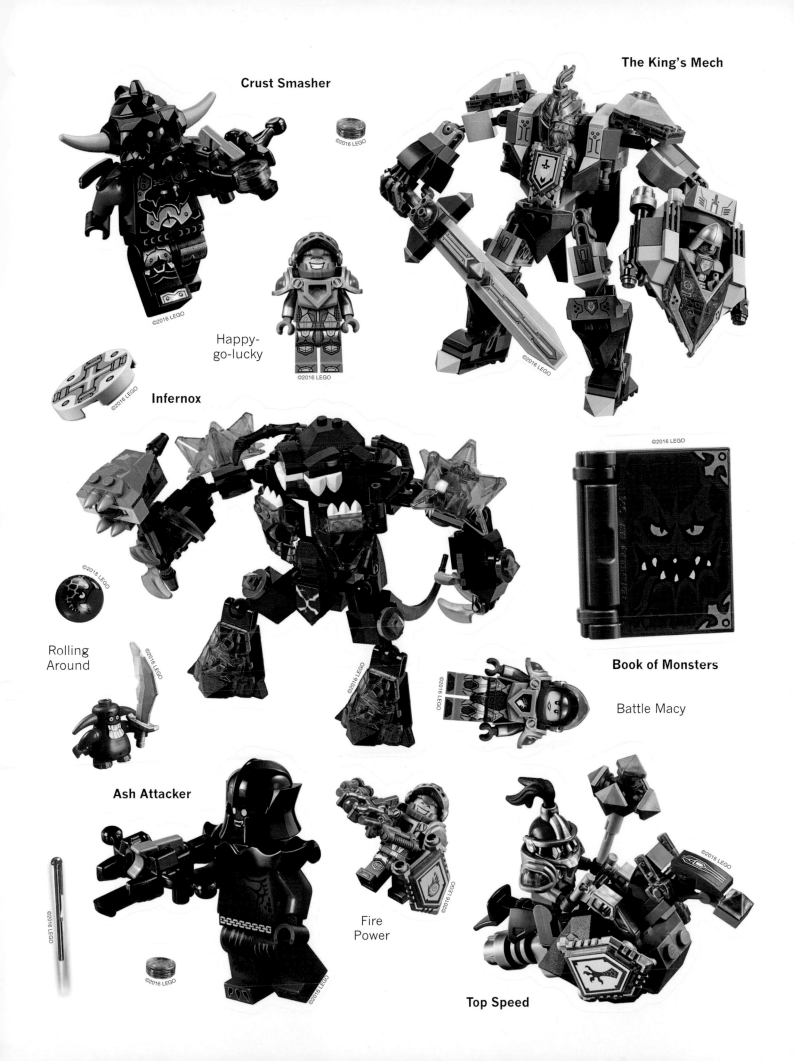

Crust Smasher

The King's Mech

Happy-
go-lucky

Infernox

Rolling
Around

Book of Monsters

Battle Macy

Ash Attacker

Fire
Power

Top Speed

Mean and Keen

Chaos Catapult

Battle Axl

Fired Up

Helmeted Monster

Knight
Cycle

Axl

Clapper
Claw

Claybot

Secret Ammo

Lava Shooter

Winged Flyer

King Halbert

Mean Monster

Globlins

In Full Armour

Cheery Lance

Bad Joke

Heroic Clay

Towering Ahead

Motoring Ahead

Lava Smasher

Bot Blade

High-speed Chase

Magic Book

Wizard Hologram

Crowning Around

Battle Powers

Blade to Blade

Two-pronged Attack

Target Practice

Fiery Enemy

Ready for Battle

Sparkks

Hover Horse

©2016 LEGO

©2016 LEGO

Soldier Support

©2016 LEGO

©2016 LEGO

Chaotic Catapult

©2016 LEGO

Bombs Away

Knight training

©2016 LEGO

Ava

©2016 LEGO

Ground Power

©2016 LEGO

©2016 LEGO

Red Globlin

©2016 LEGO

©2016 LEGO

Speedy Escape

©2016 LEGO

Mech Attack

©2016 LEGO

©2016 LEGO

©2016 LEGO

Fire Disc

Flame Thrower

Macy

Mean Magma Monster

Rumble Blade

Treasure Chest

Guard

Book of Chaos

Backlash Lightning

Airborne Aaron

Squirebot

Charge!

Mini Bot

Catapult Attack

Armed
Knight

Bots into
Battle

Full Steam Ahead

Happy Aaron

Hungry Axl

Kingly Charge

Blade to
Blade

Jestro

EXTRA STICKERS

EXTRA STICKERS

EXTRA STICKERS

EXTRA STICKERS

EXTRA STICKERS

EXTRA STICKERS

EXTRA STICKERS

EXTRA STICKERS

©2016 LEGO

EXTRA STICKERS

EXTRA STICKERS

EXTRA STICKERS

EXTRA STICKERS

EXTRA STICKERS

EXTRA STICKERS

EXTRA STICKERS

EXTRA STICKERS

©2016 LEGO

EXTRA STICKERS

EXTRA STICKERS